To Patrick, Conor, and Colleen, with big, big love.
—J.G.

To Cindy, for her love and encouragement . . .
and to Murphy, for being my Marley.
—R.C.

Bad Dog, Marley!
Text and art copyright © 2007 by John Grogan

Printed in the United States of America.

Library of Congress Cataloging-in-Publication Data is available.
ISBN-10: 0-06-117114-X (trade bdg.) — ISBN-13: 978-0-06-117114-7 (trade bdg.)
ISBN-10: 0-06-117115-8 (lib. bdg.) — ISBN-13: 978-0-06-117115-4 (lib. bdg.)

Typography by Jeanne L. Hogle
13 14 15 16 17 18 19 20

First Edition

John Grogan

Bad Dog, Marley!

MARLEY

illustrated by Richard Cowdrey

HarperCollins*Publishers*

In a little house on Churchill Road lived a very happy family.

There was one mommy, one daddy, one freckle-faced girl named Cassie, and one crawly, squirmy boy named Baby Louie. He had a giant, droopy diaper and a thumb that rarely left his mouth.

The family had two parakeets, three goldfish, and four pet crickets. But there was one thing the family did not have, and that was a dog.

"Oh please, please, please, please," begged Cassie. "Please, can we get a puppy?"

"Peas!" cried Baby Louie.

"We'll see," said Daddy.

"We'll see," said Mommy.

Cassie and Louie waited and waited until . . .

Daddy came home from work one day carrying a cardboard box.

"Hey, everyone! Come see!" he yelled.

In the box was a squiggly yellow furball with a wet black nose and ears so big and floppy, they looked like he'd borrowed them from an elephant.

"A puppy!" Cassie squealed.
"Bow-wow!" cried Baby Louie.
"This," Daddy said, "is Marley."
"Awww," said Mommy. "Look how tiny he is."
But Marley didn't stay tiny for long.

That puppy ate and he ate and he ate. He ate what was in his dish. He ate what wasn't.

He drank and he drank and he drank. He drank what was in his bowl. He drank what wasn't.

The more he ate and the more he drank, the more
he pooped and the more he peed.

And the more he grew and grew and grew.

And the bigger Marley got, the bigger
trouble he got into. Big, big, bad-boy trouble.

Marley ate the buttons off jackets and the laces off shoes.
He tipped over his water bowl and raided the trash.
He pulled the toilet paper off the roll and the turkey out
of the oven. He chewed Mommy's reading glasses and
swallowed Daddy's paycheck.

"Bad dog, Marley!"
Daddy said.
    "Bad dog, Marley!"
Mommy said.

    "Bad dog, Marley!"
Cassie said.
    "Bah boo-boo, Waddy!"
Baby Louie said.

Marley tried to be a good dog, honest he did. But everything he tried ended up bad.

He tried to make friends with the squirrels.

"Bad dog, Marley!" Mommy said.

He tried to play house with Cassie and Louie.

"Bad dog, Marley!" Cassie said.

"Bah boo-boo, Waddy!" Baby Louie said.

He tried to find a safe hiding place
during thunderstorms.
"Bad dog, Marley!" Daddy said.

One day Mommy baked cookies and left them
on the counter to cool. Big mistake.

The next day Mommy baked a chocolate
cake and put it high on top of the refrigerator.
"You won't get this," she said.

But Marley
got it. Every
last crumb.

Another time Marley jumped over the fence and came home with a giant pair of underwear. "I don't even want to know," Daddy said.

One day Marley finally went too far. The family came home from a movie to find an indoor snowstorm. There in the corner of the living room was the Abominable Snowmarley.

"Uh-oh," said Baby Louie.

"That's it," Mommy said. "That dog has got to GO!"

"Please, Mommy," Cassie cried. "Marley didn't mean it. He can't help it."

"I'm sorry," Mommy said. "I can't take it anymore."

Marley was very, very sad. *I try so hard and I mess up everything. Everything!*

Daddy put an ad in the newspaper:

Big Yellow Dog — a little crazy but with a pure heart. Free to good home.

Strangers came to meet the big, crazy, pure-hearted dog, and every one received the same royal Marley welcome.

"No thanks," they all said.

Then one day Marley proved he was right where he belonged.

Mommy was in the bedroom folding clothes when Marley started barking.

"Bad dog, Marley!" Mommy scolded. "Pipe down!"
But Marley would not pipe down. He barked and barked.

Then Mommy heard
Cassie scream, "Come quick!
It's Louie!"
Mommy raced for the kitchen.
"My baby!" she cried.

Before Mommy could take a step, Marley
raced up the drawers, leaped onto the counter,
jumped up on his hind legs—and grabbed
Baby Louie by his great big droopy diaper.
Marley would not let go until Mommy had her
baby safe in her arms.

"Good dog, Marley!" Mommy said.

"Good dog, Marley!" Daddy said.

"Good dog, Marley!" Cassie said.

"Me go again!" Baby Louie said.

Marley jumped on the floor and did the Marley Mambo.
Finally, I did something right!

"Does this mean . . . ?" Cassie asked.

Mommy looked at Marley doing his crazy dance. She looked at Cassie, then at Daddy. She squeezed Baby Louie in her arms. Finally she looked back at Marley.

"Oh please, please, please, Mommy!" Cassie said.

"Peas!" Baby Louie said.

A little smile came to Mommy's face. "This is Marley's home, and we are his family," she said.

"And we love him very much," Daddy added. "Slobber and all."

"So Marley can stay?" asked Cassie.

"Yes," Mommy said. "Marley can stay."

"Yay!" said Cassie.

"Yay!" said Baby Louie.

"Woof!" said Marley—and gave Mommy
the biggest, fattest kiss of her life.

"Good dog, Marley!"